For Jason, my forever friend
- CF
For Anna, with all my love
- BC

First edition for the United States and Canada
published in 2013 by B.E.S. Publishing

First published in Great Britain in 2007 by Simon & Schuster UK Ltd
Africa House, 64-78 Kingsway, London WC2B 6AH

Book designed by Genevieve Webster

All inquiries should be addressed to:
B.E.S. Publishing
250 Wireless Boulevard
Hauppauge, New York 11788
www.bes-publishing.com

ISBN-13: 978-0-7641-6670-9
ISBN-10: 0-7641-6670-0

Library of Congress Control No. 2007923771

Printed in China by Leo Paper Products
Date of Manufacture: March 2019

10 9 8 7 6

Aliens Love Underpants

Claire Freedman & Ben Cort

PUBLISHING

Aliens love underpants,
Of every shape and size.
But there are no underpants in space,
So here's a big surprise...

When aliens fly down to Earth,
They don't come to meet YOU...
They simply want your underpants—
I'll bet you never knew!

Their spaceship's radar bleeps and blinks
The moment that it sees
A fresh clothesline of underpants,
All flapping in the breeze.

They land in your backyard,
Though they haven't been invited.
"Oooooh, UNDERPANTS!" they chant,
And dance around, delighted.

They like them red, they like them green,
Or orange like wild pumas.
But best of all they love the sight,
Of Granny's spotted bloomers.

Mom's pink frilly panties
Are a perfect place to hide
And Grandpa's woolly long johns
Make a super-whizzy slide.

In daring competitions,
Held up by just one pin,
They dive into the long johns
To see how many can squeeze in!

They wear undies on their feet and heads,
And other silly places.
They fly undies from their spaceships and
Hold funny undies races!

As they go zinging through the air,
It really is pants-tastic.
What fun the aliens can have,
With underpants elastic!

It's not your neighbor's naughty dog,
Or his owner's funny game.
When underpants go missing,
The ALIENS are to blame!

But quick! Mom's coming out to fetch
The laundry in at last.
Wheee! Off the aliens all zoom,
They're used to leaving fast...

So when you put your underpants on,
Freshly washed and nice and clean,
Just check in case an alien
Still lurks inside, unseen!